Clarence, the Talking Giraffe
for your precious children and ours
erin kathleen, kelly hope and meghan baylee

Read books to your children
and sing them lullabies
for time will pass
and they grow up too fast
right before your eyes...

mary & justin case

Clarence,
the Talking Giraffe©

ISBN 1-890382-00-0
Library of Congress Catalog Card Number: 97-71999

...Clarence, the Talking Giraffe,
is like giving a hug to a long lost Friend...

Clarence, the Talking Giraffe

lived at the Zoo

He shared his jokes

with little folks

that's what he loved to do

The children, they adored him

and stayed the whole day through

He told them tales

of chasing whales

and other fun things to do

But one day when the zoo

was closed and the children

were not around

Clarence looked real close

and sitting on the post

was a boy name Georgie Brown

Now, Georgie looked real lonely

he sure could use a friend

Like a Talking Giraffe

to make him laugh

so he could smile again

Then Clarence walked on over

and said,

"Hey Georgie Brown...

Don't look so sad

it's not too bad

let me show you what I found!"

And he lifted the boy up in the air

with his neck stretched all the way

Over the trees

that blew in the breeze

and the clouds that were out that day

And when Georgie reached

the very top he could not

believe his eyes

There were marshmallow creams

with rainbow dreams

and chocolate lullabies

The clouds were cotton candy

there were chocolate cherry trees

The river flowed

of caramel gold

and banana split the seas

They played all day, they played

all night, they played all afternoon

Every day

they came to play

but time went by too soon

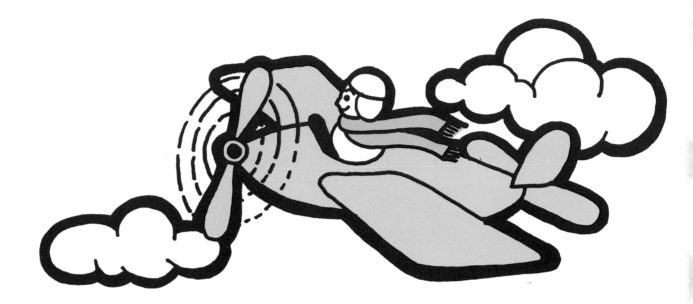

You see, you cannot play forever

and all good things must end

When little boys

put away silly toys

and these children turn into men

And it happened there one day

that Clarence lost his friend

He never said why

or even good-bye

he just did not come back again

Days turned into weeks

then months turned into years

And the Talking Giraffe

forgot his laugh

as smiles turned into tears

And the Candy Treasure

up in the sky

began to melt away

Then the story told

began to unfold

when Clarence became sick one day

He closed his eyes while

on the ground

and didn't get up that day

His bones were old

and he was not so bold

with nothing left to say

But one day when the zoo

was closed

and no one else was there

A voice came through

the Giraffe right to

and his head went up in the air

There standing at the old post

was a man named

Mr. George Brown

And he hugged the Giraffe

then started to laugh

with his long lost friend

that he found

But Clarence had grown old

and gray,

and could no longer

reach the sky

Until a little hand

came from behind the man

holding that Chocolate Lullaby

And there stood Georgie's little

boy, who could surely use a friend

Like a Talking Giraffe

to make him laugh

and suddenly Clarence

felt young again

Then he lifted the boy up in the air

with his neck stretched all the way

Over the trees

that blew in the breeze

and the clouds that were out that day

And when the boy reached

the very top

he could not believe his eyes

There were the

marshmallow creams

with the rainbow dreams

and those Chocolate Lullabies

The clouds were still cotton candy

there were chocolate cherry trees

The river flowed

of caramel gold

and banana split the seas

Then they played all day, they played

all night, they played all afternoon

And the love that they share

would always be there

and not go away too soon

... the end